METRIACANTHOSAURUS

BRACHYTRACHELOPAN

SHANTUNGOSAURUS

DRACOVENATOR

GEOSTERNBERGIA

ABELISAURUS

ERLIKOSAURUS

DIABLOCERATOPS

EOABELISAURUS

AEROSTEON

JANE YOLEN

How Do Dinosaurs Show Good MANNERS?

Illustrated by

MARK TEAGUE

THE BLUE SKY PRESS
An Imprint of Scholastic Inc. · New York

THE BLUE SKY PRESS

Text copyright © 2020 by Jane Yolen
Illustrations copyright © 2020 by Mark Teague

Library of Congress catalog card number: 2019031106

ISBN 978-1-338-36334-0

10 9 8 7 6 5 4 3 2 1   20 21 22 23 24

Printed in Malaysia   108
First edition, October 2020

Book design by Kathleen Westray

For my grandkids who are tired of
my lectures on manners!—J. Y.

To Lulabelle—M. T.

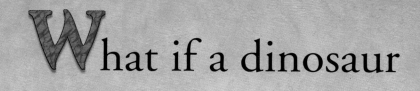

What if a dinosaur
won't be polite?
Maybe burps at the table
and starts a food fight?

Does she spit out
her broccoli
onto the floor?

Does he shout, "I hate meat loaf!" while slamming the door?

Does a dinosaur know what the word "PLEASE" is for?

Does she yell and toss books
off the library shelf,
then grab all the dinosaur books
for herself?

Does he bully his friends?
Push them off the big slide?

Does he tell baby brother,
"No piggyback ride!"

Does she dump pails of dirt in the tub? Make a flood?

Does she sassily say,
"I'm inventing
new mud!"

No,
dinosaurs
don't.

DIABLOCERATOPS

They're never that crude.
They're always polite
and try not to be rude.

They say "PLEASE" and "THANK YOU."

"I'll clean up that dirt."

"Excuse me for burping."

"I'll help when you're hurt."

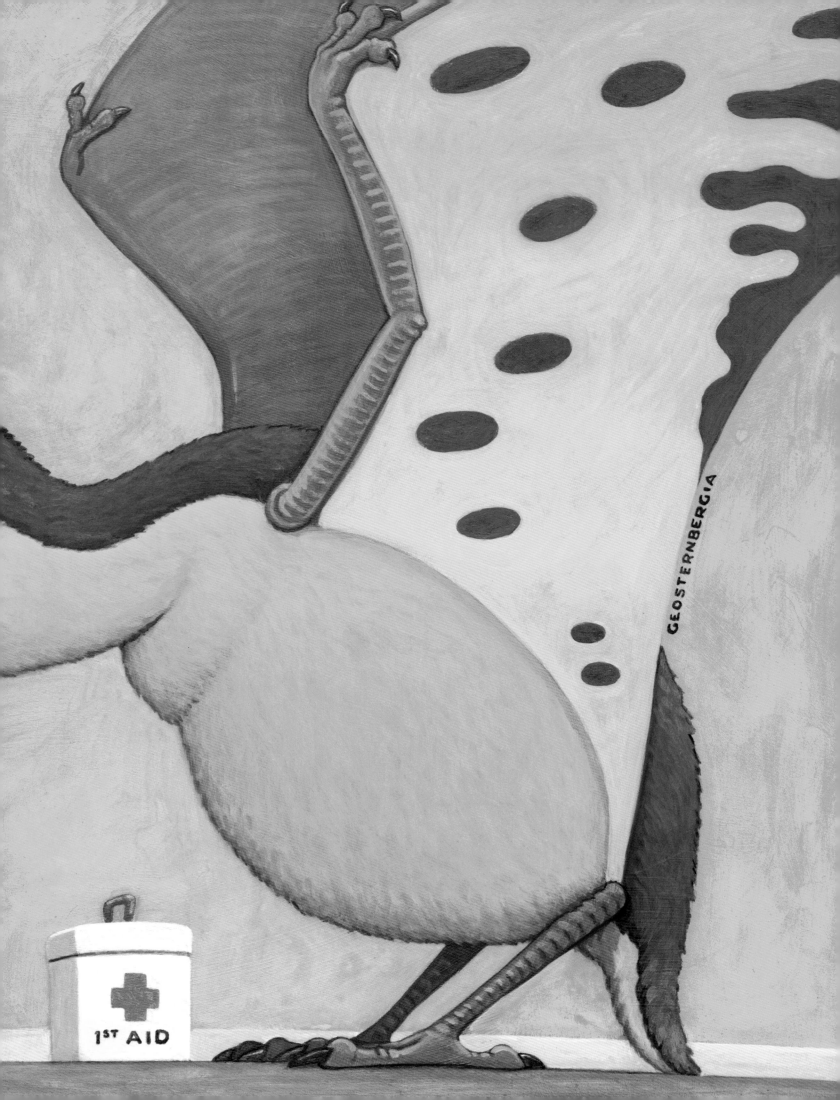

They wipe up the tables and vacuum the floors.

They share all the books
and they *never*
slam doors.

He and his friends
all take turns down the slide.

He gives
baby brother
a BIG
piggyback ride.

And after each gift,
or a favor's been done,
each one says politely,
"Thanks!

Thanks, everyone!"

Good manners galore,

my polite dinosaur.

METRIACANTHOSAURUS

BRACHYTRACHELOPAN

SHANTUNGOSAURUS

DRACOVENATOR

GEOSTERNBERGIA

ABELISAURUS

ERLIKOSAURUS

DIABLOCERATOPS

EOABELISAURUS

AEROSTEON